Northern Narratives #2

TALL TALES OF ALASKA

JUNEAU AK

A Quaint Alaska Town
with a Gold Mining Problem

W.R. Kozey

ISBN 978-1-954896-39-0 paperback
ISBN 978-1-954896-43-7 ebook
ISBN 978-1-954896-42-0 audio

Printed in United States

Cover photographs and illustrations Sam Grubitz Southeast Alaska map iStock.com/Artist Rainer Lesniewski.

Fathom Publishing Company
PO Box 200448 | Anchorage, AK 99520
Fathom Publishing.com

To my loving wife, Kaitlin.
For if it wasn't for her incredible spirit
and desire for adventure, I may have
never come to Juneau,
let alone call it home.

Contents

Acknowledgments

I would like to begin by acknowledging the Indigenous peoples of Alaska and their ancestral homelands. I want to pay my respects to all the Tribes that call this land their home and recognize the deep and abiding connections they have to this place.

I would also like to acknowledge the brave and tenacious souls who traveled north to Alaska during the gold rush seeking fortune and adventure. For it is their experiences and struggles that line these pages and without them there is no book.

Finally, I want to express my gratitude to all those who have contributed to this work, whether through guidance, support, or inspiration. This collection would not have been possible without their contributions— thank you.

How did Juneau get its name?

Many folks expect a town name like Juneau to appear somewhere down south like Louisiana or French Canada, but not in Alaska though. That is because not too many people know the town's namesake, Joe Juneau, a French prospector. And, even fewer people know that this name would be vastly different if it weren't for the signature Alaskan shot called the Duck Fart made famous by one of Juneau's oldest bars, the Red Dog Saloon.

But first, before we get into that,

you'll need a little more background on Alaska's capital city; and, to do that, we'll need to go back to the time of the Alaskan purchase. Russia had just sold Alaska to America, and at that time, Sitka was the capital. As for Juneau, it was just a small fishing village named Rockwell after the Navy's Lieutenant Charles Rockwell who had been stationed in these parts before the gold rush.

It was a fine name for that town. However, when large amounts of gold were found in the area, the place changed. It changed so much so that the United States even decided to make the quickly-growing city Alaska's capital.

But there was still one problem, Rockwell didn't have the right ring to it to attract prospectors as far north as Alaska. So, the newest gold rush town needed a new name. And it would be the townsfolk that would vote on what the new Alaskan capital would be called.

The decision came down to two

names: Harrisburg and Juneau. The two names referred to Richard Harris and Joe Juneau, the two gentleman given credit for "discovering" the area and the vein of gold that came with it.

Both men had their own ways of convincing residents to vote for them. Harris built a building downtown with the name "Harrisburg" on its side to bolster his claim. The building still stands and is situated on the corner of one of Juneau's busiest intersections—South Franklin and Marine Way—but, as we all know, the town isn't called Harrisburg. No. The town is called Juneau, and it was Joe's creativity and persuasiveness, and a little help from some liquor, that got him the votes.

As the story goes, on the day of the vote, Mr. Juneau invited all the would-be Juneauites to what is now Manila Square, the center of downtown, so that he could plead his case. However, something was off that day. And, being the perceptive man that he was, Joe picked up on it. The people seemed tense, even stressed. So, what did Joe do? Instead of making his stand in the square, he opted for a more relaxed environment. Joe asked all those that had gathered to follow him to the closest bar, to have a round on him.

Once inside, Joe asked the bartender to get the fine folks of town a beverage that would taste nice but have enough kick to give them the liquid courage to stand up to Richard Harris and name the town Juneau. The bartender poured Duck Farts, so many Duck Farts in fact that "Fart for your vote!" quickly became Mr. Juneau's new slogan. And once the townsfolk were sufficiently drunk, Joe went ahead and led them all down to town hall to cast their ballots.

Ol' Joe won by a mile and, despite some grumblings from Harris, no one could argue with the results. And the town has been called Juneau ever since.

So that's the story of how a clever and persuasive man named Joe Juneau—and a drink made of coffee liquor, Irish cream, and Canadian whiskey—changed history and gave Juneau, Alaska, its name.

Who found the gold first?

As we learned in the previous story, Joe Juneau and Richard Harris are the two prospectors who are given credit for "discovering" Juneau—and all the gold that came with it. But how did they know where to look? The Alaskan coastline is long, rugged, and unforgiving, and to stake a claim on an area is pretty much a guess. This is where Chief K̲awa.ée comes in, a man that would change the town of Juneau's history forever.

For context, Chief K̲awa.ée of the

Auk Tlingits was a respected leader and skilled hunter, known for his knowledge of the rough terrain of Southeast Alaska. And, according to the locals, one day, while out exploring the mountains, he stumbled across a vein of gold that ran through the cliff face of what is now called Table Top Mountain.

The discovery was a crossroads for Chief Ḵawa.ée, who knew right away that it could bring wealth and prosperity to his people. But he also knew that it would attract the attention of the newly arrived Americans, eager to exploit Alaska's natural resources.

When he returned to his Tribe and shared the news, an intense debate broke out about how to handle the situation. Some Tribal members argued that they should keep the discovery a secret, fearing that the Americans would find a way to take their land. Others wanted to negotiate with the Americans and try to work out a deal that would benefit both sides.

In the end, it was Chief Ḵawa.ée's decision, and despite being hesitant, he knew this discovery wouldn't stay secret long. So, he traveled south to Sitka, the territory's main hub when it was Russian, hoping to find someone who could help navigate the complex world of gold mining and American commerce.

In Sitka, Chief Ḵawa.ée met a man named George Pilz, the first professional mining engineer in the new American territory of Alaska. He showed Pilz the sample of gold he'd brought with him, a nugget the size of Chief Ḵawa.ée's fist. The mining tycoon nearly fell out of his chair.

The very next day, George enlisted Joe Juneau and Richard Harris, the now Mining Hall of Fame inductees, to travel with Chief Ḵawa.ée back to the area to investigate the claim.

On their first trip to Juneau, the two prospectors traveled up Gold Creek as far as Snowslide Gulch. And what they found stunned Joe and Richard. The gold ran right along the surface of the mountain! One could simply bend over and pick it up.

So, the two prospectors acted quickly to stake their claim before anyone else could find out. They rushed back to Sitka with a few samples and, upon seeing them, Pilz dropped everything else and ordered an immediate follow-up trip to the site—only this time, he would be coming to see for himself.

It didn't take long for Pilz to approve. He took one look at the rich deposit around Snowslide Gulch and announced that Juneau and Harris' claims had been fairly staked, and that the mining of the area should start at once.

As for Chief K̲awa.ée, he was torn between his duty to his people and his desire to protect the land. Ultimately, he remained rooted in his duty to his people, working to ensure respect for the Auk Tlingets and also the land in which they stewarded.

That said, the discovery of gold in the Juneau area transformed the region, attracting thousands of miners and fortune-seekers. And many of them found that fortune alright. During the gold rush, roughly $150 million of gold was mined in and around Juneau, which when accounting for inflation, translates to roughly $7 billion today.

That said, the legacy of Chief Ḵawa.ée and his people is still talked about—a testament to the delicate balance between ambition and stewardship. It reminds us of the importance of respecting the land and its custodians, even in the face of untold riches.

How did Juneau become the capital city?

Many of you reading this book may not remember the time when Juneau wasn't Alaska's capital city. As a matter of fact, many of you might not even remember that Alaska wasn't always part of the United States. And for those of you who fall into this category, by reading this story, you might learn a little bit about not only American Alaska, but Russian Alaska as well.

That's right, before 1867 and the

Alaskan purchase, the territory "belonged" to Russia. And Russia's center of government in the area was not in Juneau, but in the coastal town of Sitka. It was there that the Russians established their seat of power during the days of Russian-America, and it was there that the Americans initially chose to govern their new territory.

But as the years passed, Sitka's central location along Alaska's southern coastline became less important, and when gold deposits were found in 1880 along the rugged hills surrounding Juneau-Douglas, it became clear that a change might need to be made.

Because of this discovery, the region began to flourish, growing larger and more influential with each passing day. And as Juneau-Douglas blossomed into a bustling hub of activity, the need arose for a more accessible seat of government— one that could accommodate the needs of the growing population and handle the legal matters that came with it. So, the call went out to Congress and eventually a bill was drafted to move Alaska's capital to Juneau, citing the town's rapid growth and promising future.

And it was none other than President McKinley who eventually signed the Alaska Bill into law officially designating Juneau as the capital of the Last Frontier.

But the transition was not without its challenges. Governor John Brady resisted the move, claiming a number of ridiculous reasons as to why it should remain in Sitka. His first claim was that the change would destabilize the entire region. Another was that it would uproot numerous families that had already settled in Sitka. But, in reality, the only relocation that actually mattered to the governor was his own. He did not want to leave his beautiful home and the multiple business ventures he'd already established in Sitka.

This battle went on for six long years before the governor's office finally made the move to Juneau. But move it did. And with the move, came the arrival of Governor Wilford B. Hoggatt and the termination of Governor Brady. Thus, the transfer of power was complete, and Juneau's status as Alaska's capital was once and for all cemented.

But the debate over the capital's location is still far from over. To this day, residents of Alaska are still making proposals to relocate the capital. Only now they want it moved to Anchorage— the state's largest and most accessible city. But, despite many efforts, Juneau remains the location of Alaska's government.

And so, whether you've visited, or plan to visit Juneau, the country's most beautiful capital city, you now know a little more about our town's role in the state's history. For though the journey may have been long and full of challenges, the capital of Alaska will always be Juneau—a place that encompasses the very best that is the vast wilderness of the Last Frontier.

Why did
the Treadwell Mine close?

April 21, 1917, will be a day that is always remembered in Juneau. This is because it was the day that the Treadwell Mine, one of the most lucrative mines the United States has ever seen, closed down.

It wasn't because of a lack of gold, though. No. On April 21, 1917, the mine experienced a catastrophic event leading to its shafts flooding and eventually collapsing in on themselves.

The collapse occurred at around

6:30 p.m., and the impact was felt several miles away due to the sheer magnitude of the cave-in. The shock wave caused a tidal wave to rush through every inch of the mine's underground tunnel system, flooding it with seawater from the nearby Gastineau Channel.

As for how the mine collapsed, it is said there were a combination of factors. First, the mining activities that had been going on for years had weakened the underground pillars that supported the mine. And second, on the day of the collapse, there was an abnormally high tide which caused seawater to flood three out of the four mine sites, putting extra pressure on the pillars below. This led to the crumbling of the weakened pillars and the eventual collapse of the entire mine system.

And, from what I'm told, there were roughly three-hundred-and-fifty workers scheduled for work that day; however, the high tide kept most of them away. Only thirty-six men made it down into the shafts that morning and were working in the mine at the time of the collapse. Thankfully, they all made it out alive.

That said, the Treadwell Mine collapse did not go without casualties. There were a number of horses, mules, and donkeys that were used to transport ore and equipment that didn't make it back out and perished in the flooding.

Moreover, despite there not being any human casualties, Juneau's economy took a major blow. As I mentioned before, at the time, the Treadwell mine was one of the largest and most productive gold mines in the world and a significant source of employment and income for the local community.

Additionally, the collapse of the mine had far-reaching effects on the people of Alaska, as many of the men who worked in the mine were local residents and breadwinners for their families. Not to mention, the impact it had on the global gold market which was already struggling due to World War I.

Now, with all of these negative consequences, it is hard to see how any good could have come out of this awful event. But something did. The collapse led to a complete overhaul of mining practices and workplace safety standards within Alaska. Mining companies began to focus less on sheer profit and more on maintaining the structural integrity of their mines and ensuring the safety of workers.

Today, the Treadwell Mine is a popular tourist attraction and visitors can explore the remnants of the once-thriving mine. If you take a tour, they even allow you to work with some of the still-functioning machinery. And for those of you that are brave enough, you can even rappel down into the collapsed mine.

That said, just remember to heed the tide, the waters in Alaska are unforgiving.

What is the building
in the channel?

As you learned in the previous story, the Treadwell Mine was once a prominent fixture in Juneau, but since the collapse, tourists can now only visit its ruins. That said, one of the mine's ruins has become an iconic landmark in town, appearing on a number of postcards and paintings. That structure would be the old pumphouse which stands alone on the south side of Douglas Island, often surrounded by water and only accessible during low tide.

The building is rather picturesque Alaskana—a solitary silhouette jutting out of the water with only mountains and forest to complement its skyline.

However, the significance of the Douglas Island pumphouse lies less in its construction and beauty, and more in the actions of the brave souls who manned its pumps on the day of the Treadwell Mine collapse.

You see, as the story goes, when the mine collapsed and the waters began to rise, the thirty-six individuals who were scheduled to work that day were about to be trapped within its depths. But amidst the chaos and confusion, one pumphouse operator thought quickly and sprang into action, rushing up the ladder to his post to turn on the pumphouses' three pumps. At the time, the pumps were capable of removing roughly 2,700 gallons of saltwater per minute from the area surrounding the mine.

Now, of course, the pumps weren't able to prevent the flooding, nor were they able to keep up with the impending ocean water threatening the mine. And if you read the previous story, you know that the mine did eventually collapse. But, locals around town still say that it was those pumps and that pump operator's actions on April 21, that slowed the flooding just enough to allow everyone to escape safely.

And so, as the sun sets over the Douglas Island pumphouse, and you are either flying over it in a plane, or cruising past it on your cruise ship, remember that it is not simply a remnant of Alaska's gold rush glory days. Rather, it is a memorial to the courage of those who stood against the tide and refused to be swept away.

What ended
mining in Juneau?

Earlier in this collection, you learned about the glory days of the Treadwell Mine and the eventual collapse that led to its closure. This event was devastating for Juneau, of course. That said, it wasn't the end. Determined to rebuild what was lost that day, the town banded together and, later that year, the Alaska Juneau (AJ) Mine opened for operation.

In the AJ Mine's hay day, the 1930s,

it operated around the clock, employing
roughly a thousand Juneau residents
and producing ninety million tons of
gold bearing ore. Now, for those of you
who don't know what that means, those
thousand employees made up roughly a
quarter of the entire town's population,
and within those ninety million tons
of ore, three and a half million ounces
of gold were discovered, making the AJ
Mine one of the largest in the world.

But the years passed and the world
changed. And at the end of the decade,
the world was staring down the barrel of
another world war. As a result, the cost
of labor sky rocketed while the price of
gold plummeted. This nasty combination
sealed the mine's fate, and they closed up
shop in 1944.

At this point, you're probably saying
to yourself, "but why would they stay
closed? The price of gold is higher than
its ever been!" And you'd be right, at the

time of writing this story, the cost of gold was approximately $2,300 per ounce which is plenty to have folks consider re-opening the mine.

And many have. Since the AJ Mine's closure, the property has exchanged hands on more than one occasion—the most notable being the Echo Bay Mining Company which invested around $100 million before abandoning the idea.

Currently, the City and Borough of Juneau own the rights to the land and are examining the feasibility of re-opening. However, there is one rather large problem standing in its way—tourism.

In the aftermath of the mine, the town of Juneau was desperate. With one of its largest industries once again on the verge of collapse, the town needed to find ways to employ people quickly before they started to look elsewhere to live. And the answer was cruise ships.

The people in charge at the time

were smart. Knowing that Juneau is landlocked and sea-locked, they knew that the best way to get large amounts of people to travel this far north would be on a cruise line.

So, they began work on constructing deepwater ports to accommodate such large vessels. And where did they build these ports?

Well, they built them in the only place that would work, just south of town, right below where the AJ Mine used to operate. And as time has gone on, this initial port has now expanded to five ports including multiple gift shops and restaurants which service the 1.7 million cruisers traveling to the shores of Juneau every summer.

Now, no one in town is complaining. The cruise industry brings millions and millions of dollars to Juneau every year helping fund community projects and a number of other industries.

However, having grown the area south of town to cater to an influx of people, safety becomes a serious concern when talking about mining the hills just above.

And so, instead of mining the hills, the people of Juneau now mine the tourists, selling them T-shirts, hats, raincoats, and even condoms with the names Juneau or Alaska printed on them.

Nevertheless, the memory of the AJ Mine is still strong in town. Locals still talk about why it closed and the untold riches that remain in its shafts undiscovered—believing that there is still plenty of gold in the hills surrounding town.

How did the people know when the cruise ships were coming?

In the mid-1900s, Alaska was still largely undiscovered by tourists. But, as you just read, due to the one-two punch of the Treadwell Mine collapse and the economic impact World War II had on Alaska's economy, the territory found itself needing to find other ways in which to generate income for its residents. That's where the cruise ship industry comes in.

These companies saw potential in the Last Frontier's untouched beauty and sent steamships to Alaska's waters bringing people from all over the world to see the glaciers, the wildlife, and the quaint little fishing towns that dot its coastline.

Keep in mind, it was a risky business navigating the narrow channels and unpredictable weather of Southeast Alaska back then. Mainly, because the ships at the time were nothing like the massive vessels that ply the Alaskan waters today. They were small and slow, with no radar or GPS. So, there was no way to predict when they would arrive at their destinations.

This uncertainty raised issues for more than just those aboard the ships; it also created problems for the local business owners. During these early days, the locals had no idea when to open their shops for the visitors.

In Juneau though, they had a secret weapon. And that weapon came in the form of a small little dog named Patsy Ann. Now, you might be asking yourself how on earth a puppy could help shop keepers in Juneau know when the ships were going to be in port. Well, I'm about to tell you.

But, before we look at the how, let's first find out the who. Patsy Ann was a bull terrier from Portland, Oregon. And not unlike other bull terriers, Patsy was partially deaf at birth. When Patsy's owners brought the little puppy to Juneau, this impediment got worse, leaving Patsy completely deaf in both ears by adulthood.

But did Patsy let that stop her? No. Patsy hated being indoors and would always be looking for ways to sneak out of the house. Eventually, Patsy's owners allowed the dog to roam free, tired of constantly being bull rushed by their bull terrier every time they left the house.

And, from what I've been told, one of the reasons why Patsy Ann kept on fighting her way outside was because she wanted to go greet the steamships coming into port.

Despite being deaf in both ears, the puppy had this remarkable gift—she somehow knew the ships were coming down the channel long before anyone else. Some say it was because she could sense the high pitch of the steam escaping the engine. Others say she could feel the vibrations produced when waves crashed against the steamship's hull. Either way, when Patsy picked up on a visiting ship, she would dash down to the docks and start barking repeatedly, letting everyone know that visitors were on their way.

The people of Juneau soon began to rely on Patsy Ann. They would hear her barks and rush down to the docks, ready to greet the ships and their passengers.

Tourists loved the little bull terrier, too. They would take pictures with her and give her treats, and Patsy Ann became somewhat of a local celebrity in town. She was even dubbed the "Official Greeter of Juneau, Alaska" by Juneau's mayor in the mid-1990s.

But, as the years have passed, technology has improved and radar and GPS are now widely adopted, making it easier to navigate Southeast Alaska's narrow channels.

Puppies with special gifts like Patsy are no longer needed to inform folks on when the ships are scheduled to dock. However, Juneau's famous bull terrier will never be forgotten. The people of Juneau erected a statue on the docks in her honor, acting as a reminder of the humble beginnings of the cruise ship industry here in Alaska and proof of how far it's come.

Today, Juneau is a bustling tourist town that welcomes over a million tourists every year. The ships that come to port are massive, holding thousands of passengers and crew.

Every once in a while though, someone will spot the statue of Patsy Ann and take a second to read the plaque telling the story about the little puppy who helped put Juneau on the map.

Why don't they build the road?

As we learned in the previous story, Juneau has been, and still is in a lot of ways, isolated from the rest of world. But not knowing when the cruise ships are coming is one thing; it's a whole other thing to be on the mainland, yet not be connected to any sort of road system.

That's right, Juneau is unlike any other capital city in the United States because it is completely landlocked and sea-locked, meaning the only three ways to get to town are by boat, by plane, or by birth canal.

Some locals, though, keep fighting to build the road. Their argument for connection is security: security for the economy, strong and secure supply chain routes, protection against inflated living costs, and the security that comes from having Alaska's capital city connected to the rest of the state. And they're not wrong. That is why, even today, after decades of surviving without the road system, walking up and down the streets of downtown Juneau you'll see bumper stickers reading "Build the Road."

That said, on the other side of the coin, you have folks embracing the unique isolation that comes with living in a sea-locked and landlocked city. This group has found solace in the snow-capped mountains, lush forests, and tranquil waters that surround them. In fact, some actually believe that the lack of road access has only added to Juneau's charm. They think that tourists coming to visit are fascinated by the city's unique way of life and the stunning scenery that has been left untouched due to the town's "hidden gem" location.

But in all reality, the reason Juneau is not connected to the state's road system is much more practical. Although the Mendenhall Valley might appear to be flat, the ninety miles between it and Skagway are not.

The mountains along this route are surrounded by water and ice. On one side, you have the Gastineau Channel, which feeds into the Pacific Ocean. And, on the other, you have the Juneau Icefield which straddles the coastal mountain range on the United States and Canadian border.

To move forward with such a project, the road would not go around the mountains but through, requiring the majority of the length to be tunneled.

Not to mention, the areas that aren't tunneled would need to be constantly cleared in the winter due to storms and potential avalanches. As one can imagine, this would be pretty costly, eating into whatever revenue the road would bring to town.

In the end, the lack of road has not defined Juneau. Instead, it has become a unique selling point that Juneauites are proud of.

Today, Juneau remains a thriving city, one that continues to draw visitors from all over the world. And while there are still some who dream of a road connecting Juneau to the rest of the state, most folks are fine with the way it is. Because they know that it is precisely this lack of road access that makes their city unique—proving that sometimes, the most beautiful places are the ones that require a little extra effort to reach.

Who is the richest person to live in Juneau?

Of course, Juneau is a mining town; however, there are more ways than one to make money here, and any one of them could have resulted in the richest tycoon to ever walk these roads.

For instance, tourism services bring in heaps of cash. Since the perfection of the cruise liner, Juneau now welcomes over one million tourists during the summer months which supports the town's economy.

And, all those people have to eat.

With the influx of tourists, there's a constant demand for food, drinks, and entertainment. Investing in restaurants, cafes, bars, or even souvenir shops in this town can be extremely profitable.

Now, you're all probably thinking it, the richest person to ever live in Juneau was a miner. And, if you've read this far, you're probably thinking that it was Joe Juneau or Richard Harris, the miners accredited for finding the gold in town. You might even venture a guess that it was John Treadwell, the owner of the largest gold mine in the area.

Logically, these would all be very good guesses. But no, none of these sectors, not even gold mining, hold a candle to the wealth that can be accrued by finding buried treasure.

That's right, the story of the richest man in Juneau has nothing to do with tourism, hospitality, not even fishing. It is a story of adventure, fortune, and a whole lot of luck.

Now, the name of the man in our story has been lost to the passage of time, but his legend still lives on in the whispers of those who live in Juneau and the surrounding area. He was a daring adventurer, one who roamed the towering peaks and sprawling fjords of Southeast Alaska.

And, as legend has it, one day, as the sun shone down on the Taku Glacier, our protagonist decided to embark on a journey that would forever alter his future. Piloting his trusty helicopter, he plotted his course down the Taku River Pass. The route would take him between a narrow section of mountains that ends in a massive glacial ice field. On the other side, Canada.

But he wouldn't make it to his final destination. No. Fate, as unpredictable as the Alaskan weather, had other plans. A sudden gust of wind, a momentary lapse in concentration, and the helicopter plummeted from the sky, crashing amidst the rugged mountains of the Taku River.

By the grace of God, our man

emerged from the wreckage with only a few bruises, but he was now exposed to the elements in a remote location in Alaska—not an ideal scenario.

He had to find shelter quick. Luckily for him, as he surveyed the wreckage, his gaze fell upon a sight that lifted his spirits—an old, forgotten mining shaft, hidden by the unchecked vegetation overgrowth. With trembling hands, he pushed the old door open and took refuge within the mountain. With a pounding heart, he descended into the dark recess, hoping to find water, or some sort of tool that could help him survive.

He did not find either, but what he did find would turn his world upside down—buried treasure promising wealth beyond measure.

Shimmering off of what little light made it far enough down the cavern, gold shone on every surface the man could see. It was as if the mountain was made entirely of the valuable mineral.

Now, how the man made it out of the mine, down the Taku River, and back to Juneau isn't well documented. But, what is still talked about today is his reappearance. Every day, the man would return to town, pockets heavy with the weight of gold. Sometimes, he would even bring a mason jar into town with nuggets as big as baseballs!

But it was not just the gold that captured the imaginations of the people of Juneau—it was the tales of adventure and hidden treasure that weaved this story into the fabric of Juneau's folklore.

As for the man himself, years rolled by and time claimed its toll. To his family, though, it is said that they inherited a vast swath of land along the coast and the Taku River Inlet, said to be the location of the fabled gold mine that made the man rich.

However, no one, not even the family has been able to locate it; thus, it remains a mystery. Its existence known only through the tales told by locals in the area.

Is there sunken treasure
in the channel?

In the first few stories of this book, you've come to find out that there are real riches to be discovered in and around Juneau. But, up until now, all you've learned about is what was found in the ground. What about in the water? That's right, in this Tall Tale, you'll have your imaginations stirred by the legend of the SS *Islander*, a luxury steamer ship lost to the depths of Stephens Passage.

As the story goes, the SS *Islander* was

a prominent vessel in its time, claimed to be unsinkable. And in 1901, because of its claim to fame, it was entrusted with one of the largest shipments of gold the world had ever seen—roughly $6 million in gold from the Klondike being transported southward.

But, as I'm sure you're aware, we all know what happens to "unsinkable" ships. They sink. And that is exactly what happened to the *Islander*. The ship struck an iceberg or rock while sailing past Admiralty Island, which is visible from Juneau, and succumbed to the icy waters in less than twenty minutes. Forty out of the one hundred and eighty lives on board were lost that day, either to the frigid water or the harsh conditions that awaited those that made it onto the lifeboats.

Now, this loss is an important fact, but what you really want to know is what happened to the gold, right?

Well, over the years, salvage efforts

to uncover the wealth that lie at the bottom of the channel occurred regularly. Over a dozen companies have tried to penetrate the waters of Southeast Alaska, spending hundreds of thousands, if not millions of dollars without any luck.

Some were successful and uncovered fragments of the *Islander*'s cargo—a few gold bars, some gold nuggets—but the bulk of the treasure, what would equate to $1.5 billion today, remains elusive.

Locals still talk about the sunken treasure just off of Admiralty Island; however, they don't do so optimistically. Instead, the story of the *Islander* is more of a cautionary tale—one that is explained by Southeast Alaskan folklore.

According to the tales, a great octopus stands guard protecting the remaining gold within the vessel. It is said that its massive tentacles stretch across the ocean floor and around the ship, warding off all who dare to seek the lost fortune.

Despite the passage of time, this legend endures, both captivating the hearts and minds of treasure hunters, and reminding those who call this land their home of what lies hidden beneath the surface of the sea.

Thane Trail trolls ... really?

In the previous story, you read about a mythical guardian protecting riches beneath the sea. Well, this story will also aim to stretch your imagination, only this time it's not about treasure.

Just south of the bustling streets of Juneau lies a quiet area of town, Thane. Thane is secluded because there is only one way in and one way out, resulting in mostly local traffic. That is, except for those hoping to hike the Thane Trail to the Dupont dock.

The trail head is at the end of the

road and begins innocently enough, a narrow path winding its way along the coastline where the mountains meet the ocean. On a sunny day, the views are breathtaking; yet, many folks born and raised in Juneau will avoid the trail all together. They do so because of the trolls living under the Dupont dock.

Now, at first, this may sound ridiculous. There is no such thing as trolls, right? Not to mention, trolls are supposed to live under bridges, not docks! And it is definitely a dock; it was used for storage by boats housing explosives for the mine. Yet, despite all of these logical explanations, people still whisper about what awaits trespassers at the end of the Thane Trail.

As the stories go, these creatures of shadow and stone are cunning and clever. They hide beneath fallen trees and behind towering Devil's Club bushes, their grotesque forms blending seamlessly into the natural world around them. They do so, so that they can keep an eye on hikers and protect what lies beyond the trail.

What are the trolls protecting, you ask? Well, no one really knows. Some say they are nature's guardians, born from the earth itself, to guard an ancient pathway beyond the trail, a trail not to be trespassed by mere mortals. Others have a more sinister explanation. They say the trolls were once men, cursed by nature's spirits for their arrogance and greed during the gold rush, now charged with watching over a large, undiscovered deposit of gold.

No matter what their origin though, one thing is certain, locals pass down stories of the trolls to warn younger generations. And with each telling, the tales grow more elaborate, the trolls more fearsome, and the mystery at the end of the trail more remarkable.

So, if you're looking for adventure, head out to the old Dupont dock south of town. Only, if you do, heed the people of Juneau's warnings—the trolls of Thane Trail aren't to be trifled with.

What is so special about the Taku Winds?

Whether it be by boat, by plane, or by cruise ship, if you're traveling through Southeast Alaska, I'm sure you've seen bears, eagles, and even a few whales. But, have you seen the mermaids?

That's right, the seas of Southeast Alaska are said to be home to more than just giant octopus. They are also home to mermaids, mythical creatures who call to sailors to join them down on the ocean's floor. And it is from these calls where we start to see how the tales of the Taku Winds and the mermaids of Southeast begin to intertwine.

But before we get into that, you'll need to first have a basic understanding of what the Taku Winds are. These winds, fierce and wild, and known for their sudden gusts from the northeast, are a unique phenomenon that only occur in the Taku River Valley and the Gastineau Channel where Juneau is situated. The winds are more common during the colder months, November specifically, and can be strong enough to even impact flight patterns and maritime activities in the area.

Now, it isn't uncharacteristic for Alaska to have extreme weather. That is not surprising. What is though, is the fact that meteorologists cannot fully explain why the gusts are so powerful and why the Taku Winds are so unpredictable. Some say it is just the changing of the

seasons. Others claim it is the depths
of the seas that make them particularly
intense. But if you ask a Juneau-Douglas
resident, they'll tell you that neither of
these explanations are correct. Instead,
they'll tell you flat out, it's the mermaids.

You all know what a mermaid looks
like, right? It's one of those half-fish, half-
woman creatures that lives beneath the
waves, hidden from view in the caverns
deep below the water's surface.

And, according to local legend, the
mermaids of Southeast Alaska, whose
haunting melodies draw weary sailors
to their demise, mournfully wail when
the fishing boats travel south to warmer
waters in late fall, early winter, unleashing
the Taku Winds upon the land.

They say that, long ago, the mermaids
of Taku made a pact with the spirits of
the air—a sacred bond that ensured the
harmony between the land and the sea.
And, in exchange for their celestial songs,

the mermaids were granted the power to summon the winds, to shape the weather and guide the currents along the Southeast Alaskan coastline.

And so, when the Taku Winds howl through the Taku River Valley and rattle the windows of Juneau, it is not merely the result of atmospheric phenomena, but a symphony orchestrated by the mermaids of the deep. Their cries carry across the land, a sign that yet another summer season has passed, and that it will be at least six months until the waters around Juneau will once again be full of activity.

But for those who call Juneau home, the legends of the Taku Winds and the mermaids are more than just a reminder of winter fast approaching. They are a warning, reminding us to stay vigilant and to not be distracted by the land's majestic beauty, for real dangers reside just underneath the surface.

Is the Alaskan Hotel haunted?

The Alaskan Hotel has stood tall and proud in downtown Juneau, Alaska, for over a century and acts as a beacon of history and tradition for the people of the city. But there is more to the building than meets the eye; it is also known to be one of the most haunted places in the state. This is because of its long history, one that is shrouded in mystery and legend, dating back to the mining days of Alaska.

The hotel is the oldest hotel still in operation in Southeast Alaska, and has been a brothel in Juneau twice in its existence. The first time, legally as a bordello, and the second time a little less so, acting as an unpolished gentlemen's club where men in town could come to satisfy their more primal desires. And although the madam, known as "Black Mary," the woman who ran the bordello, supported a man's right to blow off some steam, she also believed in a woman's right to support herself. She often allowed girls just passing through Juneau the opportunity to "work" off their room and board while staying at the hotel.

Now, you might be wondering why you need to know about the Alaskan's previous madam, or the ease in which a woman in Juneau could find work within the hotel's walls. Well, you're about to find out—because, it is precisely these flexible qualifications that introduces us to Alice. And as a result, we begin Northern Narrative's first ghost story.

Alice and her husband came to Alaska hoping to strike it rich during the gold rush. And to do so, Alice's husband would travel great distances to prospect areas where claims had yet to be staked. This left the couple separated for weeks at a time, and during these periods, Alice stayed in their room at the Alaskan Hotel, room 219, living off whatever wages or gold her husband would bring back with him from his travels.

Now, for a time, their plan seemed to be working. Alice would wait patiently while her husband was away, and when he would return, he'd have enough money to tide her over. However, that all came to an end when some bad weather worked its way through Southeast Alaska and Alice's husband was kept away longer than expected.

Money was running low, and on the fourth week with no word from her husband, Alice became desperate. The madam of the Alaskan realized this, so she offered Alice the same deal she gave all of the ladies living alone in her hotel—turn a few tricks and you can keep a roof over your head and food in your belly. Alice was hesitant at first, but after the sixth week of not hearing anything from her husband, she was out of options. So, she took the madam up on her offer.

Business was slow at first, but it didn't take long to pick up. Soon, Alice was in high demand; and one night of servicing thirsty sailors at the saloon would pay her enough for two weeks of high class living! She had struck it rich in Alaska all right; and, after a while, she started to settle into her new-found profession, even forgetting all about her husband—presuming he'd gotten lost and died somewhere in the mountains surrounding Juneau.

But he wasn't dead though, and as the story goes, one night, Alice was, as usual, down by the bar soliciting whoever was willing to take up her up on her offer. And on this night, one unlucky gentleman accepted. She led him to the second floor and, once in the room, began her routine. She was just about to let her dress hit the floor when she was abruptly interrupted by a loud bang and the door of the room swinging open.

Wet, disheveled, and with sadness in his eyes, there stood Alice's husband, pistol in hand. Paralyzed, Alice watched her husband's hand shake as the revolver was raised. Without warning, he pulled the trigger and her would-be-lover was dead.

Alice was in shock as her husband approached her and struck her to the ground. She found her voice and pleaded for forgiveness, but it was no use.

"If you're going to be unfaithful, this is how it is going to go," he said, lifting up his pistol and putting it to her chest. And as he pulled the trigger, Alice looked up into her husband's eyes with a heart no longer full of remorse, but instead resentment. With no one around, and nothing else to live for, Alice's husband placed the gun under his own chin and finished the job.

Now, this gruesome scene was the talk of the town for quite some time. However, after a while, as often happens, folks around town started to forget about Alice and her husband. But Alice didn't forget. No. Her spirit remained trapped in the hotel, seeking revenge on any man who crossed her path.

To this day, guests of the hotel report strange occurrences like hearing footsteps in its empty hallways or feeling cold drafts on even the warmest of days. Some even claim to have seen the ghost of Alice, her figure haunting the halls around the room where she was murdered.

Of course, all of these happenings are quite frightening, but the most terrifying experiences are always shared by the male guests. Every now and then, a man will report being pushed down the stairs. Some have heard a female voice whispering in their ear, telling them to leave. But that isn't the worst, a few have even claimed to have been woken up in the middle of the night to find an invisible force pressing down on their chest, making it hard for them to breathe.

Now, despite all of these haunting tales, the Alaskan Hotel remains a popular spot for tourists and locals alike. People continue to flock to the building to experience the history and charm of the place and maybe catch a glimpse of the infamous Alice.

And if you happen to be one of these folks, I hope you enjoy your time. A word of caution, though, if you're a man, try to avoid staying in room 219.

Are there really secret passageways underneath Juneau?

In these Northern Narratives, we've talked about mine shafts, underground caves, and secret tunnels, but we've ignored—until now—the secret passageways underneath the streets of downtown Juneau. That's right, hidden beneath the bars, restaurants, and storefronts on both South Franklin and Front Street exists a labyrinth of corridors used during prohibition.

But, before we get into that, I need to explain to you exactly how this could have possibly come about, and that brings us to two major events in Juneau's history—the Alaskan gold rush and the first cruise ship traveling to Alaska.

Let's start with the gold rush. So, during the gold rush, deep mine shafts were dug into the earth pulling out all sorts of rocks and minerals, some valuable, some not. The ones that weren't so valuable, well, they ended up being discarded along the shoreline, which would eventually create Sandy Beach on Douglas Island, and the ground beneath the streets of Juneau's red-light district— Egan, Front Street, and South Franklin. The tailings from the mine were not enough to raise up downtown Juneau above the tide line though, and this is where the cruise ships come in.

Visitors have traveled north to Alaska since 1880, but as technology improved, and the boats kept getting bigger and bigger, the need for deep water docks became evident. So, the town of Juneau decided to build piles along the coastline to build out Juneau's downtown, and to accommodate the deep water docks in the heart of the city. What they didn't realize though, was that they had also created the perfect space for the illicit trade of alcohol to thrive.

To live in Alaska, it takes a special sort of person. You are constantly having to roll with the punches. And that is exactly what the people of Juneau did when prohibition made its way to the Last Frontier.

As the waters of the Gastineau Channel lapped at the pilings beneath their feet, the bar owners took matters into their own hands. With their tools, they climbed down beneath their buildings and began to construct, with wood and with brick, secret passages below town. And these tunnels, hidden from the prying eyes of the law, became the lifeline of Juneau's underground scene during the days of Alaska's Bone-Dry Law.

With each swing of the hammer, the bars of South Franklin Street and Front Street became connected by a web of passageways, a network of escape routes and smuggling routes. But the tunnels held more than just contraband. They were also a sanctuary for those seeking solace from the icy grip of prohibition. In the dim light of the underground, patrons moved from one speakeasy to another, seeking refuge from the watchful eyes of the law.

With that said, for all of its allure, the tunnels were not without danger. With each passing tide, the waters of the Gastineau Channel threatened to reclaim its territory, flooding the passages with ice cold water. Many folks lost their lives this way. They'd make a wrong turn, get lost in the darkness and be swallowed up by the sea.

But still, the people of Juneau persevered. For fifteen long years, they toed the line of legality, defying the laws of man and nature alike.

Today, as the bars of Juneau bustle with life once again, the tunnels lie silent beneath the surface, their secrets buried beneath layers of history and folklore. But for those who know where to look, you can still find their entrances—doorways into the past and the rebellious spirit of the Last Frontier.

What is the deal
with the doll museum?

Now, for most of you who've been to Juneau, you probably have no idea what I am about to talk about. First off, because nobody coming to Alaska thinks to themselves, "Hey, let's travel all the way to Alaska to spend our afternoon looking at a bunch of creepy dolls!" No. No one has ever said that; yet, there it is, hiding in plain site on the second floor of the Triangle building.

This doll museum is like no other—

a treasure trove of history, captured in the delicate forms of wood and plastic. However, this is not why Juneau's famous doll museum makes it into the pages of this series. No. That reason, my friends, is much more ominous.

But first, let's learn about the museum itself. As you step through the museum's doors, you'll find yourself surrounded by a variety of beautifully handcrafted dolls, each one somehow connected to Alaska's rich cultural heritage. You'll find anything from Alaska Native dolls adorned in traditional regalia to antique dolls from every corner of the globe brought to Alaska by hopeful prospectors during the gold rush. The collection spans continents, cultures, and centuries, offering a glimpse into the lives of those who came before us and call Alaska home.

Some of the dolls in the museum hold a special place in the curator's heart, reminding her of her own childhood days of play and imagination. The heart of the collection though belonged to a woman with a passion for collecting antique dolls that tell the tale of Alaska. And upon her passing, the collection found its way into the hands of a friend of a friend who stored them in a downtown studio until fate intervened and she hosted a simple viewing open to the public on a First-Friday.

The response was overwhelming, with folks filling the storage space to view the variety of dolls in the group. And because of the town's reaction, the would be first curator of Juneau's doll museum decided to open it up for all to enjoy.

Of course, these antique treasures attract a certain kind of customer through its doors, but what truly sets this museum apart is a small group of dolls that the museum acquired from what used to be the local brothel. The dolls were found in some of the ladies' rooms when it was closed down in 1977 by the Fire Marshal.

Upon first glance, the dolls seem innocent enough. But, as the saying goes, it is important not to judge a book by its cover.

From what I've been told, the dolls we are talking about were kept hidden from view, deep in the brothel, only brought out when one of the women were mistreated or beaten. When this would happen, under the cover of darkness, the women would pull out the dolls from storage and gather around to manipulate them and whisper incantations. With each pinprick and chant, they called upon dark spirits, requesting them to exact justice on those who had wronged them.

Now, whether you believe in magic or not, the stories of these voodoo dolls are part of Juneau's folklore. The story best being told by those who "knew someone" who'd visited the brothel back in the 1970s and have since been woken up in the middle of the night by a sharp pain in their side or a not-so-faint burning sensation.

So, when you come to visit, as you wander through the halls of Juneau's doll museum, marveling at the craftsmanship and history on display, just remember—sometimes, even the most beautiful things can give you the heebie-jeebies. And in this case, they are totally warranted.

But hey, that's all part of the fun, right?

Who painted
the eye of Mt. Juneau?

All right folks, you've learned quite a bit about Juneau up until this point, but we've yet to address a landmark in town that always seems to catch the "eye" of visitors. And that would be the eye painted on Mt. Juneau.

If you don't know what I'm talking about, next time you're in town, take a walk down to the whale statue. Only, when you go to turn, instead, gaze up at the mighty Mt. Juneau and you'll see that there's a rock outcrop that's been painted over with a great big eye. The sight is hard to miss. The giant all-seeing eye's bold colors stand out against the earthy backdrop.

Now, the reasoning behind painting the eye is a bit of a mystery in town. Some say it was the rebel spirit of an unruly Juneau-Douglas High School student. Others believe there is a darker meaning behind it, perhaps linked to a cult or secret society. Either way, no matter how you slice it, one thing's for sure—everybody's got their own theory about the eye, but no answer as to why it's there.

The mystery continues to grow when factoring in that the man blamed for painting the eye denied even being involved. The matter is still up for debate around Juneau. Some still believe in his innocence, while others say he was guilty whether he's willing to admit it or not. Regardless, the man hasn't been seen around town since his sentencing because, well, he got kicked out of town.

That's right, because Juneau is landlocked and sea-locked, it is actually possible to kick a person out of town and make it stick. And that's exactly what they did. As punishment for painting the eye, the man blamed for the deed was sentenced to ten years away from Juneau, his friends, and his family.

Now, the sentencing may have been unorthodox, but that isn't the interesting part of this story. Even after the man was kicked out of town, the eye up on Mt. Juneau kept changing. Since the sentencing, the eye's been brown, green, blue, and today it's even bloodshot!

These changes have brought on a whole new set of conspiracies about the eye. Some are saying that there were accomplices that first fateful night, and that they are the ones continuing to paint the eye in their friend's honor. Others who think the man was innocent, claim a more magical explanation, saying that the trail is impossible to get to by foot; therefore, it must have been some natural spirit providing the mountain a way to watch over the town.

Now, whether you believe in that type of thing or not, I think it's safe to say that the town was hoping that once his penance was paid, the gentleman blamed for the eye would return and shed some light on the whole mystery. But the ten-year ban expired in the 1980s and still there's been no sign of him.

So, the tale of the eye up on Mt. Juneau remains a mystery. And though we may never know the truth behind why the eye of Mt. Juneau exists, one thing's for sure—it'll keep the town curious about what the next change in the eye may be for years to come.

Who is Romeo?

I am going to nip this in the bud and start by saying no, this story is not about the member of the Montague family that made up half of Shakespeare's fated star-crossed lovers. That guy would have never been able to hack it in the untamed landscape just outside Juneau. Instead, Romeo refers to something much more Alaskan—he was a wolf.

Known for his stunning coat of thick black fur and piercing yellow eyes that seemed to stare right through you,

Romeo was a lone wolf that lived by himself in the forest surrounding the Mendenhall Glacier. He had always been a solitary wolf, preferring the company of the forest over the pack. But one day, something changed.

According to the locals, on one late autumn day, Romeo first appeared on the trail by the Mendenhall Glacier Visitor Center. Residents had heard rumors of a lone wolf prowling the woods, but nobody had ever seen him until then. At first, people were afraid of him, unsure of what a wild wolf might do if confronted. And because of these fears, people living in the area with small children argued that the wolf should be put down. They contended that he was a danger to the community and should be shot. But, Romeo had never given them any reason to do so.

Despite the panic and uncertainty that followed him, Romeo seemed to be different. He had an aura of calmness around him that was hard to ignore. He seemed to have no fear of humans and would often approach hikers and campers without any sign of aggression. Some even reported that he would play with their dogs, chasing them through the forest and rolling around with them in the snow.

News of Romeo's existence quickly spread throughout Juneau, and he soon started attracting crowds to the glacier. People would come from all over town just to catch a glimpse of the friendly wolf. Some even started feeding him, although wildlife experts discouraged this.

And for several years, this went on without issue. Romeo lived in peace, becoming a beloved fixture of the community. However, sadly, Romeo's story does not have a happy ending.

In September of 2009, he was found

dead, apparently shot by a group of serial poachers looking for a trophy pelt. The news devastated the community. Everyone had grown to love the wild wolf who had chosen to live amongst them.

Today, Romeo is commemorated by a plaque along the trail between the Mendenhall Glacier Visitor Center and Nugget Falls, acting as a symbol of the wild beauty that exists in Alaska.

That said, his story serves as a reminder of something else. It teaches us that we need to stay vigilant in protecting Alaska's natural wonders, especially from those looking to do them harm for their own selfish reasons.

What makes
Alaskan beer so good?

In Juneau, gold mining and beer are synonymous. It is this way because, before modern refrigeration, brewers in Alaska used to take advantage of the consistent temperatures down in the gold mines to help them brew different types of beer all year round. That said, this connection between mining and brewing takes on an entirely new meaning when it comes to the Alaskan Brewing Company.

The story of the Alaskan Brewing

Company, and the secret behind their flagship beer, the Alaskan Amber, doesn't start in 1986 when they opened their doors. No. To get the whole story, you need to go back over a hundred years to the peak of the Alaskan gold rush.

In 1899, three brothers traveled to Juneau from down south, hoping to strike it rich. They worked tirelessly, day in and day out in the mines, searching for gold, but their fortunes never seemed to change, and they grew increasingly discouraged.

One day, as they explored a new shaft, they stumbled upon something unexpected. In a dusty corner, they found an old, rusty metal chest. Upon opening it, they discovered a yellowed piece of paper with a recipe written on it. It was difficult to tell in the darkness of the mine, but when they returned to the surface, it was clear the recipe was for beer.

Intrigued, the miners decided to try

brewing the beer for themselves. And, to their surprise, it turned out to be pretty darn good. Some even said it was the best they'd ever had!

Word quickly spread and soon miners, fishermen, and sailors alike were flocking to Douglas Island to taste the amber ale. The miners were beside themselves. Finally, their fortunes had changed.

The three brothers decided to go into business together and opened up shop in Douglas City—a stone's throw from the Treadwell Mine. They called the brewery Douglas City Brewing Company.

The discovery of the beer recipe brought new life to Douglas City and provided the brothers with a new source of income and a newfound sense of pride and purpose. Not to mention, they got filthy rich.

Now, it still isn't entirely clear why the Douglas City Brewing Company shut down in 1907. Some say it was due to the loss of their steady stream of customers when the Alaskan gold rush slowed down. Others say that it was the brothers' decision to take their riches to warmer climates down south. Either way, that beautiful bouquet of flavors was lost to the world for quite some time. That is, until Marcy and Geoff Larson, two home brewers from Juneau, were intrigued by a tale about three brothers who found the recipe for the world's best amber ale in an old mining shaft.

It was only a matter of time before the couple dug up the records from Douglas City to find whatever descriptions they could of the beer and how it was brewed. Once they found what they were looking for, the two got straight to work. And after incorporating a few modifications to the original recipe, Geoff and Marcy produced a small batch in their garage. Upon completion, they poured each other a pint and toasted themselves on a job well done.

That said, upon taking their first sip, the two immediately recognized the beer's potential. They instantly got to work brewing and bottling as many of the beers as their home brew kit would permit. Once they were done, they traveled from Kotzebue to Ketchikan, bringing the beer door-to-door across Alaska to raise awareness and find investors.

And, after they had accrued enough funding, the couple opened the Chinook Alaskan Brewing and Bottling Company with what they called the Alaskan Amber as their flagship beer. That same brewery has since changed names and is now known as the Alaskan Brewing Company—a brewery that has won multiple awards, distributes to over twenty-five states, and has consistently remained within the top fifty craft breweries in the United States.

Now of course, Marcy and Geoff are owed a great deal of credit for building the Alaskan Brewing Company into what it is today, and putting the Alaskan craft brewery scene on the map. However, with that said, it is also important to remember where it all started, and the three brothers that traveled north to find their fortune in gold, but instead found it in amber.

Author's Note

As you come to the end of this book of tall tales, we hope that you have enjoyed the wild adventures and colorful characters that have been brought to life through the stories of the gold rush and of Alaska's capital city, Juneau.

But it is important to remember that, although these tales have been shared and passed down by locals over the years, they are not entirely factual. They are the stuff of legend and imagination, embellished with each retelling to become bigger and more outrageous than before.

Nonetheless, these stories have become an integral part of the fabric of Alaska's history and culture, and they continue to inspire and entertain new generations of storytellers and listeners.

As you come to the end of this book of tall tales, we hope that you have enjoyed the wild adventures and colorful characters that have been brought to life through the stories of the gold rush and of Alaska's capital city, Juneau.

Who's your author?

The author telling these tall tales wasn't born and raised in Alaska, but he'll tell you he's from Alaska. He'll tell you that because he's spent the last eight years of his life living in Juneau. But it wasn't the picturesque landscapes that brought him here though. No. Instead, it was an unexpected encounter in the heart of South America that made his life take this remarkable turn.

That's right, he followed a woman all the way up north, past the sixtieth parallel.

However, their initial meeting was bittersweet. Their whirlwind romance in South America only lasted three weeks because she had a job to get back to in Alaska and, at the time, he had a company to run back home. So, they said farewell and went their separate ways.

But, upon getting home, our author knew that something was different.

Something about that girl had left an undeniable mark on his heart. And, driven by this unshakable feeling, he planned a trip to visit her in Juneau.

From the moment he landed in Alaska, he was struck by the towering mountains, lush forests, and the pristine waters reflecting the azure sky above. But, if you ask him now, it was the simple moments spent with the woman he loved that left the deepest impression. Whether it was sharing stories over a crackling fire or embarking on an impromptu hike up Blueberry Hill, every moment felt like a cherished memory.

And with each passing moment they spent together, the author's resolve to build a future with her grew stronger. So, upon returning home, with unwavering determination, he sold his shares in the company and everything else he owned, and embarked on the greatest adventure of his life.

Eight years later, he's now married to the woman he met in South America, and a proud resident of Juneau. A place that has both become his home and the backdrop to his love story—the greatest story he'll ever tell.

So, if you're in Juneau, go ahead and make your way on down to the Red Dog Saloon. And if you're lucky, you might just find him there signing books and passing out pints from behind the bar—or, more likely, drinking them on the other side.